# Scary & Silly Campfire Stories: Fifteen Tales For Shivers & Giggles

Kimberly Eldredge

ISBN: 0615690904
ISBN-13: 978-0615690902

*For Mom.*
Without you, Officer Rulz would still be unwritten.

# CONTENTS

# ACKNOWLEDGMENTS

Huge thanks go out to my wonderful state of Arizona.
Many of the stories in this book take place
around Arizona.

# INTRODUCTION:
## WHY TELL CAMPFIRE STORIES?

We've all seen it, in movies and on TV: the group of campers huddled around a campfire swapping stories. But in real life, story-time seems to take a backseat to s'mores and an early bed time.

That's where this book comes in: to help you fill the gaps. It contains 15 stories that range from the scary to the silly. I've tried to include something for everybody, no matter what type of story you like.

Telling stories around the campfire is a tradition. I've found, however, that many families don't tell stories because they're not sure how. Movies always show campers huddled around a campfire enjoying ghost stories, but that usually isn't what happens in real life.

Remember, anyone can read a story, but, when a story is told, listeners (adults or children) feel a bond between the teller and themselves.

Tips to get the stories flowing:

**1. Decide on your audience**

Will a group of adults really want to listen to a ghost story? Is a ghost story appropriate for the ages of the kids you're taking camping? The plan to tell stories around a campfire is just that -- to tell stories. It's not necessary to tell scary stories to have a good time.

**2. Know your story**

If you're telling a ghost story, know the climax and know the scariest parts. If you're telling a funny story you need to know your punch line.

**3. Have a set "story time"**

When I was younger, we didn't actually tell stories around the campfire -- by the time we got back to camp, had dinner and a s'more, it was time for bed. Our story time was on the boat, when the fishing was slow and I was bored.

The key for an effective story time is a quiet setting where you're not likely to be interrupted.

**4. Invite others to share**

If you're going to have campfire stories on your next trip, you might want to let the rest of the family, or group, know you're planning it. That way, they can bring stories of their own, or at the very least, they will make time for you to share your story with a minimum of groans!

**5. Story time doesn't have to be made-up stories**

It's a lot of fun to sit around and re-tell favorite stories (ghost, funny, or just tall-tales) but it isn't a necessity. You can also gather around the campfire to re-tell your favorite family tales too. Like the time your son locked himself in the outhouse or when your daughter caught her first fish.

The real heart of campfire story time is to reconnect with your family or friends and to participate in the ancient human tradition of telling stories. Even if you're just sharing family antidotes, campfire stories should be a part of your next trip.

All purchasers of this book will also get a free bonus story. Just text the word GoCamp to 90210 to claim your free story after purchase. If you can't send or receive a text from the USA, then email me and I'll put you on the list for future releases and also send you a link to the story. The bonus story is a Mac & PC compatible .pdf file.

Feel free to modify any story to fit your audience or surroundings. And be sure to send me an email and let me know how **YOUR** latest story time went. Was it scary or silly?

Kimberly Eldredge, The Outdoor Princess
Kim@TheOutdoorPrincess.com

# Scary Stories

# LA LLORONA
# (THE WEEPING WOMAN)

*This is a Mexican folktale told across southwestern USA and northern Mexico. It is particularly chilling if you are camping (or live) near a stream or river.*

Long ago, in a little village not far from here, there was a beautiful young girl named Maria. Maria was the most beautiful girl in her whole village. But because of this, Maria was very vain. She refused to play with any of the other children, instead spending hours combing her long black hair.

As Maria got older, so did her pride and vanity. When she was old enough to have suitors come calling, she would ignore them all. No man in the village was good enough, handsome enough, rich enough for her to marry. Maria hated the village and wanted to move somewhere more exciting. Maria vowed that one day she would marry the best, most handsome, richest man in all the land and move with him far, far away.

When Maria was eighteen, such a man came to her village. He was a ranchero, a wealthy rancher, from a faraway village. The ranchero was tall, handsome, and wealthy. Maria's mother begged Maria not to seek the hand of the ranchero for he had a mean mouth and cruel eyes. But Maria could only see the expensive suits and his handsome face.

Maria used all her tricks to catch the eye of the handsome young ranchero. In no time, he was escorting her to every dance, walking with her after dinner, and bringing her gifts of flowers and perfume. After just two short months, Maria and the ranchero were wed.

Maria thought she had everything that she wanted: a handsome husband, anything money could buy, and a grand house far from the poor village where she was born. Soon, the ranchero and Maria had two beautiful children with black hair, just like Maria's.

But as the children got older, the ranchero started to pay more attention to his son and daughter than his did to his beautiful, vain wife. When he would come home from business, he would barely say hello to Maria but would rain attention on the children; bringing them expensive games and telling them stories of his travels.

Maria, he mostly ignored.

One day, Maria overheard the ranchero telling his father that it had been a mistake to marry a peasant like Maria. He was thinking of divorcing her and seeking a younger, more beautiful bride of his own class; one who had not grown up in a poor village.

Maria got angrier and angrier. She would spend hours shut in her room trying on all her beautiful dresses and combing her long black hair until it shown like silk.

One summer evening, Maria and her children were walking along the banks of the river. The river was swollen with summer rains and ran fast and deep. From behind them, they heard someone else coming up the path.

Maria was embarrassed that her children were muddy and unkempt so they hid behind a bush, just in time to see the ranchero stroll by with a beautiful young woman on his arm. The children ran out to greet their father and he swept them into his arms.

When Maria stepped onto the path the ranchero turned to the beautiful young woman and told her, "Don't mind my children, they are always playing. I'll ask their nurse to bathe them and put them to bed." And he gave the children back to Maria.

Maria was outraged that her husband had implied that they were not married and that she was nothing more than a nurse, a servant, in his household. She was furious that he didn't notice her elegant gown and her shining black hair.

As the ranchero walked away, Maria grabbed her children and threw them into the raging river.

After they had drowned and the bodies washed away, Maria realized what she had done. Overcome with grief, she tried to throw herself into the river. But her long black hair had wound itself around her neck and was caught in a bush. Maria died on the banks of the river, strangled by her own hair.

The next morning, when the ranchero found Maria's body, he ordered that she be stripped of her beautiful dress and buried where she lay, in nothing more than her white shift. But the first night Maria was in her grave, the ranchero heard a lonely voice crying out:

"Where are my children? Where are my children?"

They say that Maria walks the banks of rivers and streams, still dressed in her white shift with her black hair wrapped around her neck, crying for her lost children. It is said that if she finds a child along a river, in the night, then she will snatch the child and drown it, hoping to regain her own lost children.

Nobody ever calls her Maria. Instead they call her La Llorona, The Weeping Woman.

# NOT AFRAID OF CEMETERIES

*This story features the game of geocaching. If you're not familiar with geocaching, visit http://www.EatStayPlay.com/Geocaching for an explanation.*

There once were two friends who loved geocaching: Brian and Kevin. The pair had been on all types of adventures but their favorite types of geocaches to find were in cemeteries.

Now, technically, caches aren't supposed to be IN cemeteries so the friends would go out of their way to find caches that had actually been hidden in among the gravestones. Both boys loved how eerie and scary cemeteries could be.

When Kevin started dating Jenny, she thought that geocaching was just for nerds. And visiting cemeteries…

"What's so scary about cemeteries?" Jenny whined. "It

just a bunch of old graves and stone angels."

After accompanying Brian and Kevin on several outings, Jenny told them that geocaching was just a dumb game and that she would be staying in the car from now on.

Night was falling; a storm was coming up and the wind was whipping. The friends could see flashes of lightning out in the distance. Unable to go after the last cache, they took shelter in a diner.

"Why do you like doing this?" Jenny asked over chocolate milkshakes.

"It's creepy visiting the cemeteries. I love it when the chills run up and down my back and it feels like someone is watching me," Brian explained.

"And I love the way the stone angels seem to reach out and try to grab me," Kevin said.

Jenny just laughed. "You guys are nerds," she said. "There's nothing scary about cemeteries!"

Brian was getting pretty frustrated with Jenny. She was Kevin's girlfriend, but she was getting to be a pain in the butt. She didn't understand geocaching and she didn't get a chill at all, no matter how creepy the cemetery.

"Oh yeah, Jenny?" Brian said. "Then have you heard about the Black Angel in Shady Hills Cemetery? Legend has it that anybody who visits the Black Angel at midnight is grabbed by the statue and dragged to hell."

"Whatever!" Jenny said.

"No really," Brian said. "There's actually a geocache hidden in Shady Hills Cemetery and the geocache owner warned geocachers to stay away from the Black Angel. I'll bet that you're too chicken to go there after dark."

"I'm not scared of a stupid statue or a cemetery," Jenny said. "I'll go there tonight, at midnight, and prove to you for once and all that cemeteries aren't scary and the Black Angel is just a legend."

"You're on!" Kevin said. He was tired of Brian always giving his girlfriend a hard time. "You'll see, Brian. My Jenny isn't afraid of anything!"

The three friends waited in the diner until late. The storm had grown around them until the rain was lashing down and thunder shook the windows of the diner. Finally at 11:30, Brian got everybody in the car for the drive to Shady Hills Cemetery.

When they got to the cemetery, the storm was stronger than ever. Kevin handed Jenny his long, black raincoat to offer her some protection from the storm. As Jenny was getting out of the car, Brian grabbed her sleeve.

"You have to stay there until the church bells finish striking midnight. Here, take my pocket knife. Drive it into the dirt at the foot of the Black Angel. That way, we'll know that you actually went all the way to the Black Angel, like you said."

The rain whipped down and the thunder boomed over head. Jenny hurried away from the car into the cemetery.

11

She arrived at the grave just as the first toll of midnight rang out across the cemetery. She plunged the knife into the soil as the second toll of the bell rang out across the cemetery. As she was standing up, she though she saw the Black Angel reaching out for her.

Jenny's scream was lost between a peal of thunder and the tolling of the church clock.

She turned to run, but something was holding her back. Jenny screamed and screamed, but each scream was drowned by the tolling of the bell and the raging storm.

When Jenny didn't come back to the car, Brian and Kevin started to get worried. Grabbing flashlights, they entered the cemetery to look for her.

They found Jenny at the foot of the Black Angel statue, dead. Brian's knife had been driven through the bottom of the raincoat, pinning her in place.

But while the official report was that Jenny died from fright, nobody could explain why her rain coat had been shredded, as if by claws.

Nor could anybody explain why the Black Angel had shreds of raincoat caught between its stone fingers.

# CRY BABY CREEK

*Sometimes the best ghost stories are the ones that you tell as if it happened to you. The key to making them super scary is to relate most of the story in a matter-of-fact voice until you near the climax of the story. Then, let the creepiness be heard in your voice.*

Tulley Creek, just a bit west of here, has been known for years as Cry Baby Creek. Tulley Creek used to flow year-round, but about 15 years ago, the creek went dry. Now, it only flows once a year, on October 4th.

That's because, when I was young, Shelly Armstrong died at Tulley Creek on October 4th. Shelly had been driving home from work late one night with her infant son Jack asleep in his car seat in the backseat.

It had been storming all afternoon and Shelly was anxious to get home. The rain had made the dirt road slick and treacherous. The pot holes were filled with water and shoulders of the road were soft. Shelly had her windshield wipers on at full speed but it seemed as soon as they moved the water, the rain blurred the windshield again. Her headlights barely illuminated the road in front of her.

As Shelly approached the old wooden bridge over Tulley Creek she noticed that the creek was flowing much higher than ever before. It seemed that the bottom of the bridge was only a few feet above the raging surface of the creek.

Shelly slowly eased her car onto the bridge. Even above the sound of the rain, she could hear the bridge moan and pop. Just as she was nearly across, the bank on the far side slid into the raging waters below.

Shelly watched, helpless, as the whole bank in front of her gave way, revealing the supports of the bridge. Just as she was putting her car into reverse to back off the bridge, the bridge gave way and plunged Shelly, her car, and her still-sleeping young son, Jack, into the tumultuous waters below.

The next morning, searchers found Shelly's body 30 miles downstream. Her car had washed up in some shallows. They searched for three days, but they never found the body of young Jack Armstrong.

Now, people say that if they visit Tulley Creek on October 4th they can see the waters rise and go rushing through the creek bed. And if you go to the site of the old wooden bridge, you can still hear young Jack Armstrong crying for his mother.

I went to Tulley Creek, Cry Baby Creek, one year. I was 16 and had just gotten my driver's license. I was too afraid to roll down the windows to listen for the baby to cry, but when I drove away, on my back window was the imprint of a baby's hand.

### Story Telling Hints:

- Feel free to adjust the time frame to fit your audience.

- Change the date in the story from October 4th to be the date you're telling the story.

- If you think your audience can handle it, have a "helper" sneak away and cry like a baby at the very end. (Caution!)

# THE WOMAN AT THE BRIDGE

*This story is best told by a male, but could be modified to use a male relative of the storyteller. It is best if you replace the place names with the names of places that your audience will recognize.*

A few years ago, I was driving home on a rainy summer evening. The wind was whipping the rain so it was nearly heading in sideways and I could hardly see out the windshield.

As I was coming to the Willow Bridge underpass, a figure in white stepped out from under the bridge and raised one hand. I quickly braked and just avoided splashing the person with water from a large puddle. I rolled down the passenger window to yell but was confronted with a beautiful young woman in a white dress, soaking wet.

"Do you need help?" I asked her. After all, who would

be waiting under a bridge in a rain storm if they didn't need help?

"Can you give me a ride into town?" She answered. I nodded and she opened the door and got in. I noticed that she was shivering so I offered her my coat that was sitting in the back seat. She wrapped it around herself as I continued on into town.

"What were you doing under that bridge?" I asked her.

"My boyfriend and I were at the movies. We got into a fight and I made him let me out of the car. Thank you for picking me up."

To my discomfort, she started to cry. She pulled out a white hanky to dab at her eyes but it looked as wet as her dress.

I tried to get her to talk to me, but she just stared out the window and cried quietly. I vowed that if I ever met the lousy boyfriend who had left her under the bridge, I was going to break his nose!

My passenger shivered every now and again and pulled my coat tighter around her. I turned the heater up since I could tell she was still cold.

As we got into town, she started giving me directions to her home. But it was as if she didn't really want to talk to me since she just said things like "Turn here" or "Take the next right." Pretty soon we were on a nice street in a part of town I wasn't familiar with.

"This is my house," she said quietly. As I pulled up to

the curb, the rain was pouring down harder than ever. I got out quickly to open the door for her. But when I opened the passenger door, there was nobody there. I looked around wondering if maybe she had gotten out of the car before I had come around the car.

But there was no sign of her.

Confused, I figured that she must have hurried into the house while I was coming to open the door for her. I went up to the house, noticing that no lights were on, and rang the doorbell.

After a moment, an old woman answered the door, wrapped in a bathrobe. I was a bit startled but said, "I just saw a young lady, all dressed in white. I think she went into this house." But suddenly I wasn't sure and felt foolish for waking her up.

"That was my daughter," she said.

"I'm glad she made it home alright, then," I answered and turned to go.

"No," the woman said, "she didn't. My daughter was killed in a car accident after arguing with her boyfriend at Willow Bridge underpass. It was fifteen years ago tonight. Every year on the anniversary of her death, she signals a young man to pick her up. She tries to get home to me, but she never makes it. Wait a moment," the lady said.

She opened the coat closet next to the front door and handed me a coat. My coat. "This is yours," she said.

Stunned, I carried my coat back to my car and got in.

It was only as I turned on the windshield wipers that I realized that the coat was dry, inside and out. I reached over to touch it again and in the pocket I found a damp white hanky.

# THE BIG TOE

There once was a very poor farmer named Stan. It had been a very hard year for Stan; the frost had killed his crops, the wolves had stolen his sheep, and his only cow had been struck by lightning. Stan didn't know how he was going to survive the winter.

One evening, about dusk, Stan was out hoeing weeds in his field. As he was hoeing, he said to himself:

"Poor me! I have no meat and no vegetables. If I don't find something to eat soon, I will surely die!"

As Stan was working, he came upon something that looked like a huge toe sticking up out of the dirt. Stan raised his hoe high in the air and then brought it down hard: cutting the toe off at the ground.

He thought he heard something say "Ouch!" and run away but Stan was too busy wrapping the toe up in his handkerchief to notice. Stan hurried back to his house where he put on a pot of water to boil.

Stan used the last of his supplies to make a soup. Just as the soup was starting to boil

### PLOP!

In went the toe.

After dinner, Stan said, "Yum! That was the best meal I've ever eaten. That toe was delicious." And then he went to bed.

Around midnight, Stan heard a voice in his field. The voice was calling:

"Who has my toe? Give me my toe!"

Stan was a bit frightened, but decided that nobody knew he'd stolen the toe. He put his blanket over his head and went back to sleep.

About an hour later, Stan heard the voice again:

"Who has my toe? Give me my toe!"

But this time it sounded like it was in the yard just outside his house. Stan was very frightened but he thought to himself, "All the lights in the house are dark. Nobody knows I had that toe for dinner!" He put his pillow over his head and went back to sleep.

An hour later, Stan heard the voice calling:

"Who has my toe? Give me my toe!"

Except this time, it sounded like the voice was in the house! He heard heavy footsteps in the kitchen and the voice calling:

"Who has my toe? Give me my toe!"

The footsteps came up the stairs and the voice got louder, saying,

"Who has my toe? Give me my toe!"

Stan heard his bedroom door creak open and the voice said, even louder,

"You've got it!"

**Story Telling Hints:**

- Know the "punch line" of story well in advance. This is a perfect story to memorize and then tell around the campfire.

- When you are calling for the toe, make your voice sound as creepy as possible. Like making it more of a wail and say 'toe' as if it was 'tooooooooooooooh'

- When you say "You've got it!" jump at an audience member and reach out as if you're going to grab them.

# LAKE MARY'S CURSE

Nobody swims in Lake Mary. Nobody boats and nobody wades. Fat trout jump and splash, but even the osprey find easier prey. The town won't use it for water and the elk give it a wide berth.

Nobody swims in Lake Mary. Lake Mary is cursed.

The water is cold and deep. Even on the clearest days, peering into the waters of the lake is like looking into a frosted glass.

The legend goes that Lake Mary was once crystal clear. Fishermen always caught their limit and people boated and swam and played in the waters.

But not now. Nobody swims in Lake Mary. The waters are cursed.

So when my cousin, Justin, said that there was a treasure hidden under the water in Lake Mary I believed him. But when he said we were going to swim in the lake, dive down a buoy chain and FIND that treasure, I told him he was crazy.

"I've found a treasure map," Justin said. "I loaded my GPS with the exact spot where the treasure is. It's below the red buoy."

Everyone knew the red buoy on Lake Mary. It was the only buoy that never moved no matter how hard the winds would blow. The red buoy hadn't always been red. But it was the reason Lake Mary was cursed.

It was cold that morning. And windy. The waters of the lake were frothing and chopping at the shore. We had the whole lake to ourselves. And there, just in front of us:

The Red Buoy.

Justin waded out into the waters. It was up to his knees, it was up to his waist, it was up to his chest, it was up to his neck. Cold, cloudy water encircled him as he started to swim. With every stroke of his arms, long tendrils of algae clung to his skin like the hair of long-dead corpses.

Gasping, Justin swam to the red buoy. He floated there, clinging to it. He took a deep breath and dove beneath the surface of the lake. Hand over hand, through the murk, he swam down the buoy chain. The water pressed in around him, filling his ears and his nose. He could hardly see as he worked down the chain.

Two feet down: and the algae clung to him.

Three feet down: and thick vines pushed at him.

Four feet down: and the light started to fade.

Five feet down: he saw a glimmer of white through the gloom.

Six feet down: I've got you!

*(Jump out and grab one of your audience members!)*

### Story Telling Hints:

- The trick to this story is in the telling. From the beginning you need to make your voice as creepy as possible. The scare in this story isn't in the gruesome ending, it's in the POP! of surprise after a build-up of suspense.

# HAND IN THE DARK

Karen and Donna were roommates. Both were studying to be assistant coroners. Karen was bubbly, always smiling, and outgoing. Donna, on the other hand, was quiet, focused, and reserved. Despite their differences the two girls got along pretty well.

The only complaint Karen had was that Donna was never scared or freaked out about the things they were learning. When Karen had to spend an afternoon in the morgue, all by herself, surrounded by the shrouded forms of bodies, she made it about twenty minutes before screaming and running down the hall.

Donna had no problem and didn't seem to be bothered at by any dead people. Donna NEVER got scared.

Finally, Karen had had enough of Donna's lack of reaction. So, one evening, Karen stole the hand off a dead body they had been working on. Sneaking into Donna's closet, Karen tied the hand to the string on the single bulb hanging from the ceiling.

Then, Karen went into her own closet to wait for Donna to come home and turn on the light in her closet. Karen was sure that she'd finally get a scream out of her roommate. Karen waited all night, but she never heard Donna scream. Finally, Karen fell asleep waiting.

In the morning, Karen climbed out of the closet and started to get ready to go to class. But, she noticed that the door to Donna's closet was open a little bit.

Karen thought, "No WAY Donna came home, grabbed the string to light in the closet and WASN'T scared by the hand."

She cautiously opened the closet door...

*SCREAM really loud then wait a moment.*

Karen found Donna sitting on the floor of the closet. Dead, with her eyes open wide.

And the hand?

It was wrapped around Donna's neck, choking her to death.

# THE HOOK

Anna and Ryan were out on a date one July evening. Normally, after dinner and a movie, Ryan would drive them to a city overlook where they could sit in the car and make out. But tonight, when they got to their favorite spot, there was already a car there.

"Let's just go home, Ryan," Anna said. "I'm tired."

"Nah, come on. I know of a better spot a little farther along the road," Ryan responded. And he kept driving. After ten minutes, he slowed down and pulled off onto a narrow track that was hard to see between two large bushes.

"This is perfect, Anna," Ryan said. "Nobody will bother us here."

But Anna looked around and started to worry. This spot was a lot farther from town than they usually came and it was very secluded. Sensing her worry, Ryan

28

switched on the radio and then gathered Anna into his arms.

As they were kissing, suddenly the radio announcer interrupted the music to say:

"This is an Emergency Broadcast: William Borden has escaped from the state prison where he was serving a life sentence for murder. He should be considered armed and extremely dangerous. Borden is 6'3", 190 pounds, and has a stainless-steel hook in place of his right hand. Citizens are warned not to approach Borden but to call 911 immediately."

Upon hearing this, Anna began to tremble. The bushes looked menacing and the sound of a tree branch scraping against the window sounded like the tip of Borden's hook scratching the car.

"Ryan, let's go home. We're not that far from the prison!" Anna said.

But Ryan just said, "Stop worrying, Anna! That Borden guy isn't anywhere around here." And he went back to kissing her. But Anna wasn't that in to it because she kept listening for strange noises outside the car.

After fifteen minutes, the music on the radio stopped and the announcer came on again saying:

"This is an Emergency Broadcast. Escaped prisoner William Borden just murdered a woman as she left the supermarket. Borden slashed her throat with the stainless-steel hook he has in place of his right hand. Citizens are warned not to approach Borden but to call 911 immediately."

Anna looked out the window. It was dark and the wind was starting to pick up. Each time the wind blew through the trees, she thought she heard footsteps coming nearer. The leaves falling on the roof of the car became the sound of Borden's dry laughter.

"Ryan! I want to go NOW," Anna told her boyfriend.

"Aw Anna, you worry too much!" But Ryan leaned over and locked both doors. Then he tried to kiss Anna again. But Anna was scared and pushed Ryan away.

"Fine!" Ryan said and started the engine, backing out of the pull-off and speeding down the road.

Anna was still mad at Ryan when he pulled into her driveway. Rather than waiting for him to come open her door, she unlocked the door and flung it open. But as she turned around to slam it shut, Anna started to scream.

Hanging from the door handle was a bloody stainless-steel hook!

# Silly Stories

# THE MAGIC BIRD

One day, in a small city not far from here, a little boy was playing marbles in the dust. His name was Charlie and he was just eight years old. Charlie's family was very poor. There were five family members: Mama, Papa, Teresa, Frank, and Charlie. The whole family lived in a small house with only two rooms.

While Charlie was playing marbles, Mama and Teresa were fixing lunch. Papa and Frank were working in the field. Charlie heard Mama say, "I hope it rains!"

Charlie looked at the sky, but there were no clouds to be seen. In the field, Papa and Frank looked at the sky, but there were no clouds there either. There weren't clouds anywhere!

Mama called Charlie to come into the house to eat his lunch. On his plate there were three little beans. Charlie sighed but ate his beans. When he was done, he was still hungry. Mama handed Charlie a little bag and said:

"Take lunch to Papa and Frank in the field, Charlie. They'll be hungry." Charlie didn't move. "Now!" Mama said. Every day, when Mama wanted Charlie to take lunch to his father and brother in the field, Charlie pretended he was invisible. It never worked!

With heavy feet, Charlie slowly walked towards the field. Charlie hated taking lunch to the field since it was always so hot. And the field was far away from the house for his short, eight-year-old legs.

While Charlie was walking to the field, he heard a noise. He stopped dead, his heart racing. Fear rooted him to the spot. Cautiously, Charlie looked around. He saw a spot of yellow under a bush. He carefully pushed the branches aside and saw a yellow bird.

Charlie forgot all about taking lunch to Papa and Frank. He reached out and gently caught the bird! He was running home with his prize when he remembered he was supposed to be taking lunch to his family. Charlie looked at the bird and continued to his house. Putting the bird into a cage, he ran back to the fields.

Charlie gave the food to Papa and ran back home as fast as he could to check on his new pet bird.

There were three huge, black dogs surrounding the birdcage! The dogs had huge mouths filled with sharp teeth! Charlie was very frightened but he threw a rock at the dogs.

"Get away from there!" he yelled at the dogs and threw another rock. The dogs ran away! Charlie ran to the cage and looked at the yellow bird.

The bird opened its mouth and said:

"Thank you for saving my life! I will give you a precious gift in exchange for the gift you have given me. Your family is very poor. But, the field of your father will produce lots of food this year and every year after this!"

And in that moment, it began to rain!

To this day, Charlie and his family always have enough to eat, thanks to saving the life of one magic, yellow bird!

# TALE OF THE WHISKY ROW BRIDGE: A FAIRY TALE

This, my dears, is a Fairy Tale. Like every good Fairy Tale it has a beautiful princess in distress, a valiant but misguided prince, the good King and Queen, a wicked troll under a bridge, a fairy godmother, a giant, and an unlikely hero. But, unlike other fairy tales, this is a Real Fairy Tale, not a bedtime story. And in these Real Fairy Tales, there isn't always a happy ending, good doesn't always prevail over evil, the guy doesn't always get the girl, and sometimes, even the hero dies.

The unlikely hero in this story is a college freshman wishing for excitement in her life. Yes, *her* life, because this is a real Fairy Tale which means that the hero can really be a heroine.

Nancy Hall was of middle height, middle weight, middle class, with mouse brown hair, freckles, and brown eyes. She had just bought a cheap sandwich in downtown Prescott and was about to head out of the hot sunshine on the street into the cool darkness under a bridge that spanned the narrow stream ranning through the center of town when she heard a voice.

"Don't go down there, if you value your life," the voice said.

Nancy turned around and found herself face to face with a drunken bum.

"You see me as just a beggar," he said, the words oozing out between caked lips. Nancy wrinkled her nose in disgust. "But, things aren't always what they seem, here on Whisky Row," the bum proclaimed before launching into mad cackling laughter. "No, don't go under that bridge and chance the Troll!"

The bum continued to laugh as he lumbered away. Nancy looked again at the inviting darkness under the bridge and back again at the bum, who was rooting around in a trash can, looking for lunch. Squaring her shoulders, Nancy put her foot down on the first step. As her head was disappearing from street level she heard the bum call again: "Don't say I didn't warn you, girl!"

Under the bridge, Nancy settled down on a shred of cardboard to protect her jeans from the green mud, sandwich in hand.

Suddenly, she heard the wall across from her begin to rattle and hiss. She watched in disbelief as the wall slid away and showed the entrance to a tunnel. Nancy pondered for a moment, undecided. "Oh what the heck," she said, and headed into the tunnel.

"Hello!" Nancy called down the tunnel, which was lit by stinking, flickering torches. "Anyone there?" she added quietly.

With one last glance back at the opening, Nancy trotted into the unknown. She came trotting around a corner and nearly smacked into the Troll. Nancy stopped dead, nose just inches away from a stinking belly button. Her eyes traveled up and up and up! The Troll was huge: thirteen feet tall and nearly half that around with green grey skin the color of the mud and cruel black eyes. It was bald with a huge bulbous nose and large red mouth and it held a wicked club.

Nancy wondered why the Troll hadn't smashed her into a pulp with its club when she realized that it was asleep on its feet, with its eyes open. Nancy had no other way of explaining why the Troll hadn't moved when she came around the corner.

"Well, I don't want to wake it up," she murmured, slipping past the hulking beast, careful not to touch it. Behind the Troll there was the end of the tunnel, nothing but a smooth, circular room with several tunnels branching off into darkness.

Picking the tunnel that would take her as far from the Troll as possible, Nancy headed across the room. But, she couldn't enter the tunnel; something stopped her from entering. She stretched out her hand and pushed but it stopped dead and wouldn't enter the tunnel. Checking on the Troll, it still seemed to be asleep. She hurried to the next tunnel, but she couldn't pass into it either. She couldn't get out! No matter which tunnel she tried, Nancy couldn't get out of the circular room.

"Now what?" Nancy muttered. She glanced behind her, and bit back a yell as she watched the Troll roll his shoulders.

Nancy looked up and saw that there were words written on the wall in silver stone above the tunnel.

*Mists of time sunder*
*I am ready for wonder*
*Adventures I call*
*As I pass through the wall!*

Staring over her shoulder at the Troll, who had just noticed her, Nancy said the words in a rush. Still watching the Troll, Nancy hurried into the tunnel.

And tripped flat on her face!

"Well, now, what have we here?" A kindly voice asked as Nancy was struggling to her feet. She found herself lying on a cold stone floor staring into the gentle blue eyes of a King.

"Look, Queen Maggie, a strange warrior has heeded our call for help." Nancy struggled to sit up and found herself facing a pot bellied old king and his beautiful young wife. She was the wicked step-mother, no doubt. The Queen laughed suddenly, like gypsy bells.

"No dear, I am not the wicked step-mother but *the* mother. I am a fairy and do not age like you mortals. But, come, you are here to rescue the Prince, not listen to silly stories." The Fairy Queen had read Nancy's mind.

"The Prince?" Nancy asked in disbelief. "Isn't that supposed to be the Princess?"

"Well," the King said, glancing at his wife, "the Prince went off to rescue Princess Miranda from the Glass Giant but got caught himself. That is where you come in, dear. Off you go now." And so, Nancy found herself outside of the palace gates with a muddy road stretching in front of her and a very small pack laying at her feet. A very, very small pack.

"Now what?" she demanded, shaking her fist in frustration.

"I expect that you will rush off and do what you are told, dear." Nancy whipped around and looked at a woman who seemed to be the Queen's twin sister except for the green gossamer wings that fluttered over her shoulders.

"Are you my Fairy Godmother?" Nancy stammered in surprise.

"No, child, not *your* Fairy Godmother, but I am *a* Fairy Godmother. Now, I'll help you on your way and in return I want your first born son. Okay?" She didn't wait for Nancy's answer ("No way!") before whisking her off to the bottom of a glass mountain. An ethereal voice floated down to Nancy on the breeze saying,

"I'll be by someday to collect. And try not to get into any trouble!" Nancy kicked a rock and cursed all godmothers everywhere, fairy or otherwise.

"Hey!" Nancy yelled at the mountain. "Glass Giant! Come out and do battle!" To Nancy's surprise (although she wasn't sure why anything would surprise her now) the mountain cracked open in a shower of glass shards and the Glass Giant appeared.

Nancy gulped. The Glass Giant made the Troll look like a sweet two year old with a lolly pop.

"What do you seek, mortal?" the Glass Giant demanded.

"I seek the Prince and his lady Princess," Nancy replied.

"Correctly answer the riddle written on the mountain and you may have what ever you desire. Answer incorrectly, and…" The Glass Giant let the threat trail off suggestively as he gestured to the side of the mountain. Nancy quickly read and then re-read the riddle.

*What always tells the truth, but can be made to lie?*
*What lets nothing in but gives everything out?*
*What displays wealth but has none itself?*

"Um, the answer is," she paused.

"Yes, go on," the Glass Giant said, hefting his club.

"A wishing well!" Nancy exclaimed, suddenly distracted, spying the unmistakable well off to the left.

"Wrong answer!" The Glass Giant exclaimed.

"That wasn't my guess!" Nancy hollered.

"Too bad," said the Glass Giant. He raised his club and was about to bring it smashing down on Nancy's head when she darted away, toward the well. The Glass Giant came lumbering after Nancy, swinging his club. Nancy saw no other choice but to leap down into the well!

She did, hanging onto the rim so she could look cautiously toward the Glass Giant. With a huge swing of his club, he over balanced and sent his club crashing into the side of the glass mountain.

As the mountain collapsed into a heap of shards, Nancy noted that the Prince and Princess managed to come out unscathed. They grabbed each other's hands and darted away into the sunset.

Nancy looked down the well that she was perched inside and recognized the inside of the Troll's circular room. With a sigh, she let go of the side of the well and tumbled into the cave. The Troll was nowhere to be seen!

Nancy took off down the tunnel leading home at top speed and didn't stop until she was blinking in the sunlight on top of the bridge.

"Glad to see you made it back alive," the bum told her gravely. As Nancy watched, the bum swept off his dirty rags and was crowned in silver and blue robes and a glittering crown. "This is for your bravery," the King said, handing Nancy her uneaten sandwich. He winked and strode off.

So, my dears, that is my tale. Complete with all of the necessary parts for a good fairy tale. Now, in a Real Fairy Tale, the hero can die and things may not turn out happily ever after, but this is Whisky Row and things are seldom what they seem.

**On Whisky Row, even a beggar can be a king.**

PS: If you want to know the answer to the riddle, send an email to Kim@TheOutdoorPrincess.com with the subject line: "Riddle Answer."

## CHICKEN LITTLE

It is a fine fall day when Chicken Little is pecking the ground in the farmyard. She is just settling in to chase the grasshoppers under the old apple tree when

Plop!

An apple falls from the tree and bonks her on the head.

"The sky is falling!" Chicken Little cries! "I must tell the King; he will save me."

And off she runs to find the King.

Chicken Little is just leaving the farmyard when she encounters Gander Lander.

"Where are you going in such a hurry, Chicken Little?" Asks Gander Lander.

Chicken Little answers: "I am off to tell the King the

sky is falling! Come with me and he'll save you too." And so Gander Lander sets off with Chicken Little to tell the King the sky is falling.

Just as Chicken Little and Gander Lander are crossing the road, they meet Sheepy Weepy.

"Where are you going in such a hurry, Chicken Little?" Asks Sheepy Weepy.

Chicken Little answers: "We're off to tell the King the sky is falling! Come with me and he'll save you too." And so Sheepy Weepy sets off with Gander Lander and Chicken Little to tell the King the sky is falling.

As Chicken Little, Gander Lander, and Sheepy Weepy are crossing the pasture, they meet Brewster Rooster.

"Where are you going in such a hurry, Chicken Little?" Asks Brewster Rooster.

Chicken Little answers: "We're off to tell the King the sky is falling! Come with me and he'll save you too." And so Brewster Rooster sets off with Sheepy Weepy and Gander Lander and Chicken Little to tell the King the sky is falling.

As Chicken Little, Gander Lander, Sheepy Weepy, and Brewster Rooster are entering the woods, they meet Foxy Woxy.

"Where are you going in such a hurry, Chicken Little?" Asks Foxy Woxy.

Chicken Little answers: "We're off to tell the King the sky is falling! Come with me and he'll save you too."

"I know a shortcut to the King's palace," says Foxy Woxy. "Come with me!"

And so Foxy Woxy leads the friends deep into the woods. He points at a hole in the ground and says "The King's palace is just through there." And into the hole he goes.

Gander Lander follows Foxy Woxy into the hole. But Foxy Woxy has turned around and without a sound:

### *Bites off Gander Lander's head!*

And throws the body over his shoulder.

And then Sheepy Weepy crawls down the hole after Foxy Woxy and Gander Lander. Without a sound, Foxy Woxy:

### *Bites off Sheepy Weepy's head!*

And throws the body over his shoulder.

And then Brewster Rooster crawls down the hole after Foxy Woxy, Gander Lander, and Sheepy Weepy.

Just as Foxy Woxy goes to bite off Brewster Rooster's head, Brewster Rooster yells:

"Cock-a-doodle-do!"

Chicken Little hears this and says:

"Brewster Rooster only crows at dawn! It must be time to lay my egg!"

And off she goes to the farmyard to lay her egg, totally forgetting to tell the King the sky is falling!

# PRINCESS SASHA & THE EVIL KNIGHT

Once, a long, long time ago, there lived an evil knight named Sir Kwingsly. Sir Kwingsly lived in the Deep, Deep, Dark, Dark, Deep, Dark and Dirty Mountains. He had a passion for kidnapping queens and princesses to either make his slaves or to eat. He had his black heart set on marrying Princess Sasha, the most beautiful maiden in all the land. But, Princess Sasha was guarded by a very powerful wizard named Igor.

Never-the-less, Sir Kwingsly managed to capture Princess Sasha. She was out gathering herbs for some magic brew Igor was making, when out of the bushes jumped a troll! (Sir Kwingsly was the king of the trolls, who also live in the Deep, Deep, Dark, Dark, Deep, Dark and Dirty Mountains.) This troll was at least eight feet tall and smelled like last week's trash! The troll seized Princess Sasha and took her to the mountains.

When the horrible, smelly troll got Princess Sasha to Sir Kwingsly's lair, Princess Sasha was in tears. She was certain that the evil knight wouldn't make her his slave. Princess Sasha was certain that Sir Kwingsly was GOING TO EAT HER!!

Little did she know that a worse fate awaited her: marriage to Sir Kwingsly!

Word of kidnappings travel like lightning through the Deep, Deep, Dark, Dark, Deep, Dark and Dirty Mountains since everybody wants to know which beautiful queen or princess Sir Kwingsly has captured now. When the rumor of Princess Sasha's kidnapping spread to Igor, Igor was outraged. He sent his fastest messenger to tell Sir Kwingsly to return Princess Sasha or prepare to die.

When the messenger delivered Igor's missive, Sir Kwingsly roared in a rage of fury. The Deep, Deep, Dark, Dark, Deep, Dark and Dirty Mountains shook with his roars.

Even while the messenger was traveling to Sir Kwingsly's cave in the Deep, Deep, Dark, Dark, Deep, Dark and Dirty Mountains, Igor was assembling his army. Hard on the heels of the messenger, Igor's army marched toward the Mountains.

When Sir Kwingsly saw the army approaching, he called to his greatest weapon, Spike the Dragon, and told him to destroy the advancing army.

Igor didn't even realize that Spike the Dragon was circling around to attack the army until the bravest knight in Igor's company, Sir Wimpsly, charged the dragon. His lance was pointed at the dragon's foul heart. The lance hit its mark... bold and true. And the dragon Spike was dead.

The army began cheering. But even as they celebrated Sir Wimpsly's victory over Spike the Dragon, an army of trolls came thundering down the mountain. The battle for Princess Sasha was on!

Both sides lost blood, but Igor was using his wizardly powers to restore his wounded so they could continue fighting. Troll met Knight in an epic struggle. But without their greatest weapon, Spike the Dragon, the trolls quickly lost heart.

Suddenly, a white flag was raised! The trolls surrendered.

Princess Sasha rode down the mountain on a lovely white horse to meet her benefactor, Igor. Princess Sasha and Igor returned to their home in the woods, never to hear from Sir Kwingsly or his nasty trolls again.

**Moral of the story:**
- Don't gather herbs without a companion
- Only live where there are no mountains
- Princesses rule and trolls drool

# THE WOODEN FLUTE

Once upon a time there was a little village that was completely overrun with rats. The villagers had tried everything to get rid of the rats: poison, cats, hawks, and more. But nothing worked. They were completely overrun with rats!

"If we don't get rid of these rats soon," said the Mayor, "we will all have to move away!"

That evening, as the villagers were sleeping in their beds, the moon shown down as the fog crept in among the houses. And as it billowed around the statue of the King in the center of the town, the fog became a tall, thin man in a long grey cloak. The man peered at the sleeping village and fingered his plain wooden flute.

In the morning, all the villagers gathered in the square to look at the stranger. He ignored them all until the Mayor stepped up to him and said,

"How have you come to our town?"

The stranger looked down his long nose at the Mayor and replied, "I come with the night and the fog and the moonlight."

Then the Mayor said, "Who are you?"

And the stranger answered, "I am The Piper!" and he flung back his cape. "The moon and the fog have whispered to me that this village is overrun. Pay me three sacks of gold and I will take this plague with me."

The Mayor was desperate to have his village rid of rats and so he agreed. The stranger told the Mayor and the villagers that they were to go to bed like normal that night and in the morning the deed would be done.

As the Mayor lay in his bed, trying to sleep, he heard a haunting tune drifting through the village. He fell asleep with the eerie music in his ears. In his dreams he saw The Piper walking through billowing fog in the streets of the village. He saw rats pouring from every house in the village to run behind The Piper as he piped on his wooden flute.

The Mayor settled into a deeper sleep, content and knowing his rat problem would soon be over.

In the morning, the Mayor and the villagers met in the center of the village. The Piper held out his hand and said, "I have done my side of the bargain, now pay me the gold."

But the Mayor refused saying, "You've done nothing!

Just this morning a rat ran across my kitchen floor. I won't pay you anything!"

And The Piper said, "On your heads be it then!" And he disappeared in a billow of fog.

That night, the Mayor's wife was the first to fall sick. As the villagers started dying, one by one, the Mayor thought again about what The Piper had said:

"I will take this plague with me."

The Mayor sincerely wished he had paid The Piper the three sacks of gold. He would pay anything now to rid his village of The Black Death.

# DON, THE CLEVER COOK

Once upon a time, there was a smart young cook named Don. In the country where Don lived, an ugly, evil Troll had captured the beautiful Princess Laura and was holding her hostage in his cave.

Princess Laura's father, the King, had sent all of his knights, one-by-one, to defeat the Troll and rescue Princess Laura. But the Troll bested each knight and made a feast of their bones.

Then the King sent each of his wizards, one-by-one, to defeat the Troll. But the Troll bested each wizard and made a feast of their bones.

Finally, Don, the cook, asked the King if he could try to defeat the Troll and rescue Princess Laura. The King said, "Don, if you defeat the Troll and rescue the Princess, you may marry her and have my kingdom when I am gone."

So Don packed up his trusty soup pot, got onto his little white mule and rode to the Troll's cave. At the mouth of the cave, Don made a small fire. He filled the pot with water, put it over the fire to boil and sat down to wait.

Pretty soon, the Troll came to the mouth of the cave. Before the Troll could grab Don and make a feast of his bones, Don stood up and said:

"Oh great Troll! It is known far and wide that you are among cleverest of all Trolls for you have stolen the fair Princess Laura. I have come to make you a soup that will the smartest Troll in the land!"

And since Trolls are very vain about being clever, the evil Troll didn't grab Don and make a feast of his bones. Instead, the Troll growled: "And just what is this soup?"

Don said, "It is Stone Soup! See this stone? It makes the best soup in the world and when you eat it, you will be the smartest Troll. First, I need an onion."

The Troll was being clever and asked, "Why do I have to give YOU an onion?"

Don said, "Because if it is MY onion, then the soup would only work for me. Now, I need an onion!" And into the pot went an onion.

"When will it be ready?" demanded the Troll.

"In a little bit," said Don. "It just needs some carrots!" And into the pot went some carrots.

"When will it be ready?" demanded the Troll.

"In a little bit," said Don. "It just needs some potatoes!" And into the pot went some potatoes.

And a bit of beef.

And a handful of barley.

And a pinch of salt.

Finally, the soup was simmering and the Troll was starting to drool. Don looked up and him and said, "It's almost ready! Now, I just need to add the final ingredient: the Stone!" And into the bubbling soup went the stone.

The Troll was getting excited at the idea of eating soup that would make him the cleverest Troll in all the land.

"The soup it almost ready!" said Don. "I should just taste it to make sure that it's done."

But the Troll didn't want Don to eat the soup and become clever. So the Troll grabbed the bubbling pot of soup and swallowed it all. The Troll started choking. He had swallowed the hot, boiling stone! In a moment, the Troll was dead.

Don walked into the cave and rescued Princess Laura. They returned to the King and were married. When the King asked Don how he had defeated the Troll, Don just said, "I make a mean pot of Stone Soup!"

# BILLY & THE OFFICIAL POLICE OFFICER RULE BOOK

Officer Roy Rulz was the most stubborn officer on the whole police force. No matter what, he insisted on following every single rule, even when they didn't make any sense! To make matters worse, he insisted that everybody else follow all the rules too!

The problem was, Officer Rulz was very forgetful and had to keep going back to his Official Police Officer Rule Book to double check all the rules. He even had to re-read simple rules like:

'No hats inside buildings.' Or 'All police uniforms are blue.'

All the children on the block knew that Officer Rulz thought rules were very important. But, they also knew that he was very forgetful since he would verify rules in his Official Police Officer Rule Book like:

'No school on Saturdays.' Or, 'Don't honk at people in a crosswalk.'

The children were getting tired of Officer Rulz always interrupting their games to remind them of The Official Rules. One little boy, Billy, decided that it was time to give Officer Rulz a taste of his own rule-loving medicine.

On his way home from school one Tuesday, Billy "accidentally" bumped into Officer Rulz, causing him to drop his Official Police Officer Rule Book. Quick as a flash, Billy switched the Official Police Officer Rule Book with his math book. He just put the cover of the Official Police Officer Rule Book on his math book and handed it back to Officer Rulz.

"I'm so sorry, Officer," Billy said and handed back the "rule" book.

Billy stayed up late that night writing up his own version of the Official Police Officer Rule Book. He was almost late for school because he had been up so late!

Billy had to hurry through the crosswalk on his way to school. Luckily, Officer Rulz was still waiting outside the school. Billy bumped into Officer Rulz again and was able to switch the books back.

Now the fun would begin!

The children knew something was different after school when they saw Officer Rulz reading his Official Police Officer Rule Book and scratching his head. They overheard Officer Rulz saying:

"I don't remember a rule about wearing yellow socks every Wednesday. But if it's in the Official Police Officer Rule Book, then it must be true!"

Sure enough, the next day, Wednesday, the children saw Officer Rulz wearing bright yellow knee-high socks with his official blue police uniform!

Then, after school, they found Officer Rulz waving his arms and arguing with the school bus driver.

"It says so right here in the Official Police Officer Rule Book," Officer Rulz said. "All school buses have to go to the ice cream shop on the way home from school!"

Everybody was excited to find out what new "rules" Officer Rulz and the Official Police Officer Rule Book would come up with next.

'Serve root beer floats to all the school children on Mondays' was a big hit with Billy's classmates.

'Buy the soccer team rocky road sundaes after every loss' made the team happy. (Especially since they hadn't won a game all season!)

'Teach square dancing at the Retirement Home Thursdays at three' was a special favorite.

And 'Wear a funky hat every Friday' got lots of giggles across town.

But the children knew the game was up when Officer Rulz started barking like a dog at his boss, Police Chief Hill, at the annual Meet Your Police Chief day at school.

"Give me that rule book!" Police Chief Hill

demanded. He thumbed through several pages. "What is this?! Where did you get this rule book?"

"That's the Official Police Officer Rule Book you issued when you hired me, Chief," Officer Rulz said. Only it sounded like:

"Woof! Woof! Ark! Grrr! Woof!"

Police Chief Hill glared at Officer Rulz. And then he glared at Billy.

Police Chief Hill knew exactly what had happened as soon as he looked in Officer Rulz's Official Police Officer Rule Book because he recognized Billy's handwriting. Police Chief Hill recognized it because Billy's full name was William Robert Hill: the Police Chief's son.

Police Chief Hill wagged a finger in Billy's face and said, "You have two days to get this all sorted out, Son, or I'm taking away your birthday until you're 35!"

Billy gulped. That night, he laid awake tossing and turning. How could he fix the Official Police Officer Rule Book so Officer Rulz wouldn't be so silly? And what about Officer Rulz's stubborn love of rules? Or his forgetfulness? Billy didn't know what to do!

As the sun rose that morning, Billy was more and more worried. Then, he got a call from his cousin, Stanley, who lived in the next county. Stanley was a great inventor. The only problem was that he would invent things that nobody really needed: like a toaster that would butter your toast for you or a hair dryer that also sang the Star Spangled Banner.

"Heard you've got a bit of a problem with a rule-loving-stubborn-forgetful Police Officer, Cuz!" Stanley said. "I think I can help!"

Turns out, Stanley had been working on a pair of reading glasses that would also improve memory. Since Officer Rulz loved to read his Official Police Officer Rule Book it would be simple to have him read it through the new glasses and then he'd remember what he read!

But there was just one problem:

Billy and the children didn't LIKE the old rules from the Official Police Officer Rule Book. They liked the rules that Billy had created in the NEW Official Police Officer Rule Book!

How could Billy keep the new, fun Officer Rulz and his funny rules without having his birthday cancelled until he was 35?

Billy had Stanley send him the reading glasses. But, for the second night in a row, Billy didn't sleep. He just tossed and turned. It seemed he had half his problem solved but he didn't really want to go back to the old, boring, rule-loving Officer Rulz.

The next day, the day of Billy's deadline, he was sitting at the breakfast table when an ad in his father's newspaper caught his eye:

**FOR HIRE:**
Recreation director for after-
school program. Applicant must
be able to follow written
directions and plan fun
games for kids.

An idea began to form in Billy's mind...

After school, Police Chief Hill called Billy and Officer Rulz into his office. He made Billy stand up and explain what had happened. Officer Rulz was shocked that Billy had marked out and changed around his copy of the Official Police Officer Rule Book.

***How could anybody do that to a RULE book?!***

It was time for Billy to put his plan into action. The first thing he gave Officer Rulz was the pair of memory-enhancing reading glasses Cousin Stanley had invented.

The second thing Billy gave Officer Rulz was a new rule book called The Official Rules to After School Games.

Then, Billy gave Officer Rulz the keys to his new office as Official Recreation Director for the City!

Even though Police Chief Hill had to hire a new Police Officer, everybody was much happier.

Officer Rulz (who is now called Director Roy) gets to

follow rules to his heart's content. And, because of his special reading glasses, he even remembers them!

Billy makes sure to provide a new copy of The Official Rules to After School Games to Director Roy at least once a month. (Billy makes up the games and their rules himself!)

And all the children in the neighborhood have a zany, fun Recreation Director: Roy Rulz.

# 7 TIPS FOR TELLING SCARY STORIES

**1. Know Your Story**

A campfire is NOT the place to be reading your story for the first time! If at all possible, don't READ your story at all, but recite it from memory for maximum dramatic effect.

**2. Matching the Details**

Stories are scarier when they happened HERE or close to here rather than on the other side of the country. Feel free to modify the details so the story seems to be set close to where you are telling it.

For example, if you'll be telling 'La Llorona', then feel free to move the setting of the story to a river or lake near where you live or where you are camping. Trust me, it's much scarier to say the river behind our campsite here in Michigan rather than some river in Arizona!

It's also very scary if you can make the story happen to you or somebody that your audience members are familiar with, like maybe a great-aunt or -uncle, the neighbor down the street, etc.

### 3. Practice Makes Perfect!

Practice telling your story in advance. That's especially important when there is dialog that you need to get right or a "punch line", like knowing when to scream. A lot of short stories have a very simple plot like:

- Car breaks down outside creepy, lonely house
- Man enters house and spends the night; makes friends with elderly hosts
- Man goes to town for tow truck
- Tow truck owner says the house burned down 50 years ago
- Returns to house and finds his jacket untouched among the rubble of the house

Now, that plot is simple enough to remember easily, but as 5 plot points, it isn't very scary. That's where you need to practice it to make it scary!

You'll want to make the story seem natural as well. Like when you're relating the family story of when you went fishing and fell in the lake.

### 4. They've Got To Trust You

You know how there are some people that you just believe and others that have no credibility at all? Well if you want your story to scare, then refrain from jumping out and grabbing people, yelling boo, etc. Be "in character" as somebody who not only has something scary to tell, but who is also a bit scared themselves.

### 5. Sow Seeds of Scary Well Before Story Time

If you can, start prepping your audience earlier in the day. You'll want them to be a bit scared long before the campfire is lit and you start to spin your tale. Good, non-descript creepy things are:

- rubbing your arms and saying you just got a chill
- saying that you feel like somebody/something is watching you
- pointing out scary things in the landscape like dead trees or ominous rocks

You can also point out landmarks that might factor into scary stories later like a dead tree or a decrepit building.

### 6. Set The Stage

There are two types of campfire stories:

1. The type that are spontaneous
2. The type that are planned

If you and your audience already know that scary stories are on the menu for the evening, then you can't really set the stage. But if nobody knows you're going to tell a scary story…

You'll have spent the day setting the stage for something creepy to happen. Now, you just need to start mentioning things like: "Something scary happened to my cousin near here." And then leave it alone.

Stories can be doubly scary when the storyteller is a bit frightened and seems hesitant to bring it up.

### 7. Be Ready For The End

Some stories lead up to being scary and end funny. Or you jump out and grab an audience member and everybody know the story was just for fun.

But some stories lend themselves to a lingering sense of unease. With stories like that, you can just trail it off into being eerie or say something like "And nobody every found out what happened to Agnes."

That can scare your audience more when their imagination picks up where your story left off.

# ABOUT THE AUTHOR

Kimberly Eldredge is a third generation Arizona native. She graduated from the University of Arizona with a degree in Creative Writing. She has been writing all her life and has been published in poetry journals, short story anthologies, and regional travel magazines.

In addition to writing scary and silly campfire stories, Kimberly also writes a blog at TheOutdoorPrincess.com with topics ranging from camping to fishing, cooking to geocaching.

She is also fluent in Spanish and has written several children's stories in Spanish.

Kimberly lives in Chino Valley, Arizona.

Made in the USA
Middletown, DE
22 March 2017